For my darling kai

First published in 2002 by Macmillan Children's Books
a division of Macmillan Publishers Limited
20 New Wharf Road, London N1 9RR
Basingstoke and Oxford
Associated companies worldwide
www.panmacmillan.com
This edition produced for The Book People Ltd
Hall Wood Avenue, Haydock, St Helens WA11 9UL.

ISBN 0 333 96621 X (HB)
ISBN 0 333 96622 8 (PB)

Text and Illustration copyright © 2002 Jane Cabrera
Moral rights asserted

1 3 5 7 9 8 6 4 2

A CIP catalogue record for this book is available
from the British Library.

Printed in Belgium by Proost

The Polar Bear and the Snow Cloud

by Jane Cabrera

TED SMART

There was once a polar bear whose only friend was a fluffy white snow cloud.

He loved the cloud,
but he wished for a friend
he could play with.

The snow cloud felt sorry for
the polar bear, so he decided to
make him a friend.
  Very carefully, he dropped
snowflakes down into the
shape of an owl.

The polar bear was very happy.
  "Maybe he will play with me,"
he thought.

So the polar bear threw a snowball at the owl. It landed with a soft squelch on its head. But the owl did not move or hoot because it was only made of snow.

The next day it had melted away.

The snow cloud tried again.
This time he made a big whale.
"Maybe we can swim and splash
together," thought the polar bear.

So the polar bear jumped into
the water and swam towards the
whale. But it just floated away
without a sound. The next day
the whale had melted away.

The snow cloud tried again. This time
he made a seal. The polar bear took
her a fish as a present.
"Maybe she will be my friend,"
he thought.

But snow seals don't eat fish,
so the polar bear sadly took the
fish away and ate it on his own.
The next day, the snow seal
had melted away.

The snow cloud tried one last time.
He dropped snowflakes slowly down
into the shape of a reindeer.
   "Perhaps she will play hide-and-seek
with me," the polar bear wondered,
and off he went to hide.

The polar bear hid for a long time.
But the reindeer never moved.
The polar bear knew that, like
all his other snow friends, the
reindeer would just melt away.

The next day, as the sun rose,
he saw another polar bear.
"He won't be real," he thought sadly.
"He'll just be made of snow."

He was just about to walk away
when a snowflake drifted slowly
down onto the new polar bear's nose.
And the new polar bear . . .

let out an enormous
sneeze . . .

ACHOO!

"You're real!" gasped the polar bear. "Will you play with me?" And he did. They played tag and hide-and-seek, and the snow cloud dropped snowflakes for them to chase. And the polar bear was very, very happy.